The Santa Slaughter

A Very Merry Murder Mystery, Volume 1

Rachel Beattie

Published by Rachel Beattie, 2022.

THE SANTA SLAUGHTER

First edition. November 30, 2022.

Copyright © 2022 Rachel Beattie.

ISBN: 979-8215053430

Written by Rachel Beattie.

Chapter One

I blink, hardly able to take in the awful scene before me. It's horrible. Worse than I imagined. I can't believe I have to be seen in public like this.

"Well?" I can hear the laughter in my so-called friend Jeremy's voice and can picture him sitting patiently on the edge of my bed, waiting to see what the obnoxious garment-bag contained. Nothing good comes from red and green spandex. "You can't hide in there forever, you know. Maggie Pritchard is expecting you at the Hot Chocolate Hut in less than an hour."

I take one more look in the full-length mirror and wince, turning to the side. It's even worse than from the front and I try sucking my tummy in, which just makes me look weirdly deformed. Not to mention uncomfortable. I sigh and reach for my lipstick, outlining my bow lips in bold, bright red. *When in doubt, wear red!* I smack my lips together and make a kissy-face at the mirror but it doesn't do much to improve my reflection. I'm still a thirty-two-year-old, soon-to-be divorcee taking the only job I can get at short notice to pay the bills my charming ex-husband landed me with when he left.

"Don't laugh!" I warn Jeremy, as I wriggle into the skirt that comes with my red-and-green onesie and thank the Lord that something is going to help conceal my hips. The ruffle hits me at precisely the wrong place but by this point, I'm committed. There's no going back. I squint at my name badge before pinning it in place. *Icey Sprinklecakes*. Maggie has *got* to be kidding. Taking one last look at myself in the mirror, I fluff my brown curls, grateful that at least one thing looks good today, and step out of the en-suite into my bedroom where Jeremy is waiting. "Well?"

"You...look...nice." The effort he's making not to laugh is practically turning him purple and in the end, worried he's going to pass out, I roll my eyes.

"Go on. I know you're desperate to mock me. Just do it now, when we don't have an audience."

"Well, that isn't *elf* bad! I mean, it takes a whole lot of *elf*-confidence to wear something like that but I'm glad to see you still believe in your*elf*."

"Ha ha." I shove my phone into my purse and slide it over one shoulder, hustling Jeremy towards the door. "Are you done?"

"Now, now. Don't be *Grumpy*!"

"Grumpy is a dwarf," I remind him, but he doesn't seem to hear me. He's still fighting back laughter.

"I'm sorry, I couldn't stop myself. But honestly, this isn't so bad! At least you aren't going to be the only elf in the grotto."

"You know, you're right." I shoot him an icy smile - living up to my elf-name - and force my words through gritted teeth. "Me and two teenage cheerleaders. What a trio we'll make." I tug my skirt down, wishing it was just an inch or two longer. "I am twenty years too old and twenty pounds too heavy for this gig, and I get two walking, talking assistants to remind me of that all day, every day. Remind me why I said I'd do this?"

"Because you love Christmas." Jeremy follows me downstairs and grabs the jacket he left on my sofa. "Because you have an extra supply of community spirit this time of year." He spies the pile of red-stamped *overdue* notices and tries to pretend he didn't. "Because you need the money?"

"Because I need the money," I agree, sliding my own coat on carefully over my costume. Not for the first time, I am grateful for my long mac which covers me from neck to ankle. Only my shoes - green felt, with an actual bell on the pointy toe - give the game away. I frown down at them, wondering if I can substitute my sneakers but before I can make the switch, Jeremy's spotted something else he can't help but comment on. I love him dearly, but goodness me, he's nosy.

"Hey, Merry, what's this?" He's reached past my pile of unpaid bills to another stack of papers I've been studiously ignoring. He cranes his neck to read the first line then whips his head around to glare at me. "You didn't sign these yet?"

"No." I glare back, and he drops my unsigned - and, honestly, unread - divorce papers back onto the table where I'd left them.

"Why not? Neil left. He's gone. And it's not like you want him back, right?"

I don't answer quickly enough for my overprotective guy-friend, because his glare becomes concerned in one swift moment and he's looking at me with those sad puppy eyes that make him – objectively speaking - one of the cutest guys in Silver Brook.

"No, I don't want him back," I say, hoping my voice sounds more convincing to him than it does to me. I don't. I *don't.* When your husband announces he's met someone younger and prettier and more successful than you the day before your tenth wedding anniversary when you have a huge party planned with friends traveling into town from all over the country, well, you don't just forgive and forget. Especially not when it later transpires he's drained your joint checking account and left you severely in the red on a whole bunch of bills you didn't even know were due. "I don't want him back," I say again, putting a bit more vehemence in my voice and satisfying Jeremy that I'm not going soft in my old age. "But that doesn't mean I need to sign the divorce papers right away." I sniff. "It's Christmas. Nobody gets divorced at Christmas."

"Right," Jeremy smirks, which somehow makes him even more handsome. Man, I hate that. "They wait until January, the seasonally-appropriate time to emancipate yourself."

"Hey, I don't need emancipating." I wave my hand, gesturing to the empty front room. "Look at all this emancipation I am enjoying. And I didn't need to sign a darn thing to get it." I roll my eyes. "Now, are you coming with me to the Christmas Market or what?"

"I am coming with you." Jeremy beams, looking far more enthusiastic than he has any right to be. "There's a cute girl running the fir tree stall that I want to get to know a little better..." He winks and I roll my eyes. At least one of us is going to have a happy Christmas this year.

"In that case, you can drive." I thrust my car keys at him and gesture to my jingle-bell feet. "I can't feel the pedals in these."

My so-called friend is still laughing when we pull into the parking lot in the center of downtown Silver Brook. "Downtown" implies a whole lot more than there really is to Silver Brook. There is precisely one main street, creatively called, wait for it, *Main Street,* and right now it looks busy, but that's only because it's lined with the festive fake-log-cabin stalls which make up the annual Christmas Market. From Thanksgiving to New Year, we do most of our trade in the great outdoors, regardless of sun, wind, rain, or snow. I risk a glance at the heavy clouds overhead and wonder just when the predicted blizzard is going to arrive.

"So, are you coming for a drink?" I ask Jeremy as we climb out of the car. My teeth are already chattering and I wrap my arms around my torso, dreading how cold I'm going to feel when I have to take my coat off and it's just thin lycra between me and the winter weather. The Hot Chocolate Hut has a cute wood-burning stove in one corner, but that's about as far from Santa's Grotto as it's possible to get.

"Trees first." Jeremy tosses me my keys. "I'm on the hunt for the perfect spruce."

I'm not rising to that and say goodbye, picking my way carefully past the line of bustling market stalls until I reach the largest of them all - Maggie's Hot Chocolate Hut. Usually busy at her cafe, the Jitterbug Junction, Maggie splits her time at Christmas between this temporary venue and the Silver Brook landmark at the other end of the street. I don't know how she does it, or whether it's worth the effort, but as she always pays for Silver Brook's popular Santa's Grotto out of her own budget, allowing all the funds raised to go to charity, I can't fault her. She's got prime real-estate this year, too. Slap bang in the middle of Main Street, between a stall selling candles and one selling freshly baked cookies. I inhale deeply, relishing the sweet, cinnamon scent, and step into the hut, making a beeline for the fireplace and waiting for the feeling to come back into my fingers and toes.

"Good morning, sunshine!" Maggie bustles over, beaming at me.

"The names *Sprinklecakes*," I say, in my best scots brogue. "*Icey Sprinklecakes*."

"Here you go." She nods, approvingly, and thrusts a cup of steaming hot chocolate my way. "Shaken, not stirred."

"Thank you!" I wrap my fingers around the mug, grateful for its warmth, and glance up at the sound of voices. Angry voices.

"Ivy...honey...!"

"Don't *honey* me! I thought we agreed -"

"I know, but this time -"

Santa - or as I know him the other three-hundred-sixty-odd days of the year, Bill Barraclough - follows his wife into the hut, stopping short when he sees me standing there.

"It's for charity," he says, catching my eye. "Right, Meredith?"

"What?" Ivy turns to glare at him, then spots me and her whole demeanor changes. She pulls herself up to her full height and offers me a tight-lipped smile. "Good morning, Meredith, dear. I see you've got yourself roped in this year, too. I like your..." Her gaze sweeps over me, at last settling on my feet. "Shoes." She turns back to her husband, all the warmth vanishing from her voice. "We'll finish this later."

"You have a good day too, sweetheart!" Bill calls, pulling the jacket of his Santa suit on over the plain white t-shirt he's wearing. He already has a beard, and I notice him fluff it absentmindedly with his fingers as he watches his wife stalk away.

Awkward...

I've been in enough married-couple-rows to know that the last thing you want when you're bickering with your spouse is an audience, so I turn away to enjoy the last of my hot chocolate and let Bill finish getting ready in peace. I'm staring out at the bustling crowds and everyone seems to be in a good mood. Carols are playing somewhere, the scent of cinnamon is in the air, and even I can't deny the Christmas Spirit is pretty strong around here. In everyone, that is, except for Peter Stalker. I hear him before I see him, striding out of his book shop with a face like thunder and marching right up to the Hot Chocolate Hut ready to pick a fight with Maggie. Fortunately, she seems to be ready for him.

"Good morning, Peter!" she says, all charm. "I've just made a fresh batch of cocoa. Do you want some?"

"No, I do not *want some!*" he yells, thrusting his hand out so fast it's a miracle he doesn't knock the tray Maggie's carrying out of her hand. She skips backward, lifting the tray and its contents safely out of the way and I'm in awe of her quick reflexes.

"Then what do you want?" Maggie asks, sweetly.

"I want to know what in God's name you think you're doing here."

Chapter Two

"Serving hot chocolate."

Maggie is completely unfazed by Peter's thinly-veiled rage and he is momentarily stunned into silence.

"Are you sure you don't want any? It's very good!" Maggie is pushing her luck, now, and I'm watching in horrified fascination until she catches my eye. "Isn't it, Meredith?"

"Oh! Yeah. Yes." I take a quick sip and promptly choke on it. It takes me a minute to stop coughing but eventually I manage it and croak out a proper answer. "Very good."

"I'm sure it is." Peter has managed to regain his equilibrium. He shoots me a look and turns back to Maggie, folding his arms across his front and glaring at her. "But why do you have to do it right in front of my store?"

Ah. Light dawns and I finally grasp what's got him all riled up. He raises his voice and says each word slowly just to make sure that everybody hears him and understands how difficult our being here is making things for him.

"You're blocking people's view of my store. Nobody is going to fight their way past this place to get to my front door. Every hot chocolate you serve is costing me book sales."

"I'm sorry to hear that," Maggie says. Her smile doesn't drop for a second. "Perhaps you'd like to advertise a few of your books here? We could dedicate a table to you and encourage people to step inside to view more of your stock."

"You want me to display my books *outside*?" Peter shakes his head. "And who will pay for the copies that get damp, or - or

-" He looks at the thick, dark hot chocolate and pulls a face. "Sticky."

"I guess you're just going to have to trust your customers will still manage to find their way past us to your door, in that case." Maggie's smile is still in place but I can tell from the tense note in her voice that she's getting tired of this argument. I finish my drink - now only really *lukewarm* chocolate - and look around for somewhere to stash my empty mug. I sneak past them, exchanging a look with Maggie that I hope Peter doesn't spot. He doesn't, but the movement does make him notice me, and he does a swift double-take, before theatrically rolling his eyes.

"And as for that thing!"

Ouch.

I freeze in place, ready to argue that I certainly don't look that bad when a noise stops me. A weird, snorting, snuffling noise. I turn my head, realizing that Peter wasn't talking about me at all, but something I hadn't noticed until that moment.

"Oh, wonderful!" Maggie beams, thrusting her tray at Peter who's so surprised he takes it, before shaking his head and placing it noisily down on a nearby table. "You made it!"

Maggie strolls right up to the reindeer - that's what Peter meant by *that thing* - and throws her arms around its neck. The animal snorts and tries to pull out of her embrace and that's when I see he has a slim rope leash around his neck that's held tightly by a tall, good-looking man standing about two feet away.

"Careful!" he jokes, stepping closer and rubbing the animal on its long nose. "Fred hasn't had his dinner yet."

Maggie steps back and we all watch as the reindeer handler reaches into the back pocket of his jeans and pulls out a handful of reindeer treats. He holds his hand out and the animal noses into it, greedily chomping away.

"What a good boy you are!" Maggie says, and the reindeer handler grins.

"Why, thank you, Ma'am!"

"Oh, you!" Maggie giggles and pats him lightly on the shoulder, and I hear the whispered *oh, please!* from Peter that perfectly echoes my thoughts on this little interaction.

"Excuse me," I say, realizing I'm squandering a very good opportunity to slip away.

"Hey! Are you working at Santa's grotto?"

No, I'm just dressed like this because I think it looks good... I clamp my mouth shut to keep from sharing the snarky comment out loud and instead plaster a smile onto my face.

"I am."

"Great. You might as well take Fred with you, then."

"Fred?"

"Fred Astaire." The reindeer handler holds out the rope towards me and I stare at it, nonplussed. "*Dancer*, get it?" He grins and I stupidly find myself grinning back, although my smile soon falters when I make sense of what he's suggesting.

"Absolutely not. Nope. Nuh-uh. I'm not working with - with that." I remember how affronted I felt to be referred to as a *that*, even though I wasn't, and add a sheepish "reindeer" onto the end of my sentence. Fred sniffs and I'm pretty sure it hasn't endeared me to him any.

"Well, you guys are why I brought him over here. Fundraising, right? For the children's hospital?"

Peter lets out a cackle of laughter at this, and I realize he's still standing there, watching our little play unfold the way I watched him face off with Maggie a few minutes ago. I turn toward him, my brow furrowing in annoyance.

"Do you have some problem with us raising money for charity?"

"None at all," he says, striding back towards his bookshop. "But if I were you, I'd keep an eye on Santa around all those collection buckets." He shakes his head, muttering irritably as he slips out of the open side of the hut. "I still don't see why you have to block *my* shop...."

"Ahem." The reindeer handler clears his throat and when I look at him, he's still holding Fred's leash out to me. He smiles and I notice for the first time how cute he is. My hand makes a motion toward the leash but I stop it in mid-air.

"Let me check with the other volunteers!" I scurry off towards the back quarter of the Hot Chocolate Hut that's been turned into a cozy Santa's grotto hoping I'll find someone else who can take charge of Fred-Astaire-the-reindeer and collide with my mirror image. Only, a younger, skinnier, blonder mirror image. Two of them.

"Hey!"

"Watch it!"

"Sorry." I regain my balance and lean down to offer a hand to one of the two teenaged elves I just knocked to the ground. Melissa - I think that's her name - lets me help her to her feet then gives me the kind of look that could curdle milk. I ignore her, and fix a beaming smile on my face, pausing to straighten my name-tag. "I'm Meredith, but I guess you'd better call me *Icey* while we're at work." I chuckle, but neither Melissa nor her friend seems to find me very amusing.

"I'm Jessica," the friend says. "And this is Ella."

"Ah." *Close.* "I guess we're going to be working together! Where's Bill - I mean Santa?"

The two teens give me identical shrugs and turn back to their phones, making it clear they're done with me.

"I don't suppose either of you has any interest in reindeer...?"

Honestly, it's like I never said a word. Neither one of them looks up from their screens, and in the end I give up, squeezing past them a little further into the grotto in hopes I can persuade Santa to come care for his own reindeer. No such luck. Bill's nowhere to be seen, but he's left his hat sitting on his chair waiting for him to come back. I spot an open box of wrapped candy canes sitting on the floor next to Santa's chair. Me and the other two elves are supposed to have easy access to them for handing out to everyone who puts a donation in our buckets. I bend at the waist, trying to get a good grip on the box but it's a lot heavier than I realized.

"Excuse me, ladies!"

I hear a smooth male voice and then a twin chorus of giggles and realize, too late, that Fred and his keeper have given up waiting for me to come back. I wriggle around, trying to lift the box and straighten before handsome-reindeer-handler-guy walks in and gets an eyeful of my derriere but the corner of the box is caught on something and instead of giving way, momentum yanks me forward, sending both me and Santa's chair crashing to the ground.

"Meredith?"

I can hear a note of amusement in that voice that I know only too well and I groan, wishing there was some place to hide. It isn't handsome-reindeer-handler-guy at all, but the one man in all of Silver Brook I did *not* want to have to deal with today. The familiar face of my obnoxious ex-husband appears above me and he grins.

"Do you need a hand?"

Chapter Three

I scramble awkwardly to my feet, leaving the box of candy canes where it sits, and hurriedly regain enough of my composure that I can shoot my ex-husband the sort of withering glance our months-long separation has allowed me to perfect.

"What do you want?"

Neil's smile falters but he forces it back into place, quirking one eyebrow roguishly at me.

"I want to see Santa?"

"Well, if you find him, tell him he's late." I reach into the candy cane box, pull out two handfuls, and push past Neil into the outer area of the grotto where I can see my two fellow elves. Zany Angelnose and Nutella Jollysocks are both now wearing their name-tags and I decide *Zany* and *Nutella* are far easier names to remember than...whatever they actually were. They are both cooing over Fred Astaire, who is enduring rather than enjoying the attention. Sadly, his handsome handler is nowhere to be found. "Here you go!" I say to the girls, passing them each a couple of candy canes. "For when the kids arrive."

"Those kids? The ones who are already here waiting for us to let them in to see Santa?"

I look to where Zany is pointing and my eyes widen. Sometime in the last five minutes the empty street filled up with fidgety children wondering out loud when we're going to change the sign from *Santa is busy in his workshop, come back soon!* to *Santa is so happy to see you!*

"What time is it?" I ask, thrusting the rest of the candy canes into Nutella's arms and leaning back into the little room I've just left, in case Bill has somehow magically found his way into his seat. I practically collide with Neil, who has taken it into his head to follow me and I decide to kill two birds with one stone. "I'll go find Santa," I tell the girls, who nod vaguely at me and turn back to pet the reindeer. Taking Neil by the arm, I haul him outside after me, my eyes scanning the crowd for a hint of Bill's broad, red-coated frame.

"So, Merry..."

Again I can hear the smirk in my ex's voice and I try to ignore it.

"Nice outfit. This is a whole new career for you, huh?"

"It's a job," I say, circling the outside of the Hot Chocolate Hut and finding all sorts of people but not the one man I'm looking for. "I've got to pay all those bills you left me somehow."

"Actually, that's kind of what I wanted to talk to you about." Neil lays his hand on my shoulder and I flinch.

"I don't have time right now," I tell him, continuing my search until my eyes fix on a bright red hat with a bobble on the end. "Fantastic! At last. Bill! I mean, Santa!" I call, waving at the figure who turns at the sound of my voice. I frown. It's definitely Santa, but this man is a bit taller than Bill. He's slimmer, too, and I'm pretty sure that beard he's wearing is fake.

"Can I help you, young lady?" The not-Bill Santa pulls his beard down to his chin and I recognize George Montgomery, another of Silver Brook's retired older gentlemen. *Why is he dressed as Santa? No, I don't want to know.* I shake my head, clearing the confusion in my head to bring my focus back to my task.

"I'm looking for Bill. He's supposed to be our Santa today, only -"

"He's gone AWOL?" George's eyes gleam with possibility. "Yes, well, I did warn Margaret that might happen. *Man of the Year* or not, he's hardly the most reliable man you might have hired." He lets go of his beard and it snaps back into place almost painfully. "If you need a stand-in..."

"We're good, thanks." I don't think I have the mental bandwidth to cope with a pair of dueling Santas today. I vaguely remember Maggie telling me there was another candidate for the gig this year but that she'd gone with Bill as he'd been her Santa for going on ten years now and always did a great job. *It'd be nice if he was around here to do a great job right now!*

"Merry."

Neil's still following me and with a groan of frustration, I turn around to glare at him.

"What part of *I don't have time right now* don't you get? I'm busy." I gesture to my outfit. "Do you think I'd be out here dressed like this if I didn't have to be? And if I don't find Santa - the one I'm looking for, I mean - there are going to be a lot of disappointed kids out there. Not to mention a drop in donations to the children's hospital, and that's not happening this year. Not on my watch." I straighten my name badge like it's a sheriff's star and stomp off, ignoring the jaunty jingle of the bells on my shoes that somewhat undermines the message I'm trying to convey.

"Fine!" Neil shouts after me. "Well, come find me when you think you can squeeze me into your busy schedule!"

I bite down hard on my lower lip, fighting the urge to turn around and kick our argument into an all-out row. *What gives him the right to follow me around today? Can't he see I'm busy? He's the one that got me into this mess when he started fooling around with that idiotic Shelly woman, and - and -* Striding through the milling crowds helps me to work through some of my frustration and I finally catch sight of Bill in his Santa suit, his head bent close to a man I don't recognize. Whatever they're talking about seems kind of intense and for a moment I wonder whether I should disturb him, but then I think of the kids and soldier on. I needn't have worried. Bill spots me before I even get close and he straightens, saying a hasty goodbye to his friend and turning towards me with a grin.

"Meredith! Or, I'm sorry, it's *Icey Sprinklecakes* today, isn't it?" He winks at me. "Something the matter?"

"Your public awaits!" I tell him, pointing towards the long queue of children that is now snaking down the street.

"Goodness!" Bill glances at his watch. "Yes, I see it's time we opened up the grotto." He comes over all chivalrous and offers me his arm. After a moment's hesitation I take it, but to my surprise, he doesn't walk back around the hut with me but steps straight up to the back of the makeshift structure, pushing open a door I've never noticed before that ushers us straight into the grotto. He makes his way to his chair, fumbling around for his hat and making himself comfortable before shooing me out into the entryway. "That's right, *Icey*! Send in the first of the boys and girls and I'll start checking them off my list! *Ho, ho, ho!*"

Chapter Four

The morning passes in a riot of children giddy on sugar and excited to see Santa - or one of his authorized "helpers", as one particularly serious-looking little boy informs me in a low enough voice that it won't reach his toddler sister, who is so busy ogling Fred Astaire she's oblivious to everything.

"That's right," I tell him, with a wink. "Just like me. We all work for the *real* Santa."

The little boy's eyes widen and I can see a hundred questions welling up in his little brain, so I'm only too happy when he reaches the front of the queue and I can usher him deeper into the grotto, past Zany and Nutella - I still haven't got a handle on their non-elf names - who are involved in the sort of whispered conversation that has nothing to do with the North Pole.

"The queue could do with some managing," I say, trying not to come over all *Mom* on them. They both execute perfectly timed eye-rolls but do at least step outside the cozy interior of the grotto and I turn to smile at Bill. "This young man has been waiting ever so patiently to see you, Santa!"

"Ho ho ho!" Bill beams at me, then beckons the little boy closer. "And what's your name, young man?"

"Matthew." The boy pushes his glasses a little further up his nose and looks as if he's coming up with a question or two that even the real Santa might struggle to satisfactorily answer.

"Why don't you tell Santa what you want for Christmas, Matthew? I'm going to go grab our camera and then we can take a nice photo to show Mommy and Daddy. Did you want your sister to be in it with you?"

Matthew shrugs in a way that wouldn't have looked out of place on my teenaged non-helpers, and I decide to see if I can tempt his tiny twin away from the reindeer with the promise of a candy cane.

"Nutella!" I call to the taller of the two elves, the one who's got our camera slung over one shoulder, oblivious to the fact that it really ought to stay *inside* the grotto. "Nutella!" It takes me three tries before I realize that isn't her name, and hiding my embarrassment I tap her lightly on the shoulder. She lets out a shriek and I feel a hundred pairs of eyes turn my way. "Can I - can I get the camera?" I ask, pointing to it. The teenager laughs awkwardly, embarrassed at her overreaction, and slides it off her shoulder, holding it out to me. Her eyes are still a little wide and I can see, despite her laughter, that she'd been properly frightened. She blinks, and her old blank expression is back in place. I frown, wondering if I'd imagined it. "Are you alright?" I ask, but Bill's voice makes its way out of the grotto, calling me back.

"Now where has that Icey Sprinklecakes got to?" A pause. "*Icey!*"

"That's my cue!" I say, turning towards Fred Astaire, who's still standing there enjoying the admiration of a little crowd of toddlers and their moms. My eyes narrow until I spot the handsome reindeer handler and I realize Fred Astaire isn't the only thing the moms are admiring.

"So, do they take a lot of care?" One mom asks, tugging thoughtfully on a silver snowman earring. "The reindeer, I mean." She giggles.

"Well, we only have one." The handler reaches into a leather pouch he has slung around his hips and pulls out half a carrot he holds in the flat of his hand for Fred to take. "He's living with my sister in Monroe Cove until she can find him a more permanent home." He winks. "But she was happy to loan him to me to spread a little Christmas cheer, and I'm never one to look a gift-horse in the mouth. Or in this case, a gift-reindeer."

There's a chorus of enthusiastic laughter and I swallow a groan, spotting Matthew's little sister and crouching down next to her.

"Hey, honey!" I pass her a candy cane. "Your big brother is about to have his photograph taken with Santa. Want to join him?" I look around, trying to match the little girl to one of the mothers in the crowd but nobody seems to be paying us the slightest bit of attention. I straighten, but a quick survey of the Hot Chocolate Hut doesn't seem to have any stray parents. I feel a tug on my lycra knees and bend down to see that the little girl is clinging to me, holding her hands out in an imploring gesture to be picked up. Fairly sure I'm about to be accused of child abduction and determined to fight it with my *just doing my duty as an elf* defense, I scoop the little girl up, holding her neatly against my hip. "Where's your Mommy?" I ask her, but she's far more interested in my camera. I frown, but as nobody's come hollering at me to put their daughter down, I decide the very least I can do is get this photograph taken. Maybe Matthew will know where his parents have got to. "Come on, sweetie. Let's go see Santa."

I hurry back into the grotto, and Matthew's sister starts squirming right as we reach Santa's throne. I frown. There's something wrong with this picture. There's Matthew, patiently hanging on to his pick from the present barrel. I put his sister down on her own two feet and she wobbles towards him. But Bill? He's nowhere to be seen.

"Where's Santa?" I ask, checking sticky toddler fingers didn't do any lasting damage to the camera.

"He just stepped outside for a minute," Matthew says, in the kind of voice that suggests he's quoting Bill verbatim on that.

Just stepped outside for a minute? I inwardly rage. *When you have a child in here with you and a dozen more still queuing up outside?* Our lunch break isn't for another quarter-hour yet.

"Are you two ok to wait here for a moment?" I ask, looking at Matthew for confirmation. He's tilted the present barrel onto its edge so his sister can reach inside and get her gift, but when he catches my eye he hurriedly straightens it. "Here," I say, reaching down into the box next to Santa's throne. "Have a candy cane." I grin. "I'll be right back, and then we'll get this photo!" My smile slips as soon as I turn away, and by the time I fight my way into the outdoors, I'm ready to really tell Bill off. Matthew might be weirdly grown up for a little kid, but he's still just that. A little kid, who waited patiently to see Santa, and doesn't deserve to be ditched so Bill can take a phone call, or...

Thump.

My foot catches on something that sends me sprawling onto the ground. I scramble back upright, my palms stinging, and look down to see what tripped me. I don't remember any obstacles lining the path earlier. My heart stops as I see Santa - Bill - stretched out on the ground in front of me. For one crazy moment, I think he *just stepped outside for a minute* to take a nap and I open my mouth to tell him he shouldn't be lying in the street but then I realise he isn't napping at all. His eyes are wide open, staring up at the sky but seeing nothing. And the pool of red that's spreading out from underneath him isn't his coat. It's blood.

Bill is dead.

Chapter Five

"Here. Drink this."

Someone hands me a cup of Maggie's hot chocolate and I take it, lifting it to my lips before I remember to say thank you.

"I can't believe he's de-e-e-a-d!"

"And it happened here! Right here! Omigosh can you imagine if the murderer was *here*? *When we were here?!*"

The two teenagers I seem to have become responsible for are both sobbing into my lap and I absent-mindedly shush them, still holding my drink.

After I discovered Bill's body, things started moving really fast. So fast, I can't even remember a lot of it. I'm pretty sure I screamed. Either way, people came running, people who know things like CPR and how to preserve a crime scene. *A crime scene.* I still can't believe that's what I stumbled into. And to think, I was furious with him.

So was somebody else, evidently.

I shiver, sloshing hot chocolate over the side of my mug. I put it shakily down on the table in front of me and go to wipe my sticky hands on my costume when someone stops me.

"Hang on."

I look up and realize the guy who handed me the hot chocolate in the first place is now holding out a sealed packet of wet wipes. I blink stupidly, trying to place him.

"I'm Rob," he says, opening the packet and fishing one of the wet wipes out. He passes it to me and I take it, wiping the sticky mess carefully from my fingers.

"Rob." It's definitely the first time I've used his name, but at last, my muddled brain clicks into gear. "The reindeer guy?"

"Rob the reindeer guy." He nods, peering past me as one of the two teenagers straightens.

"Where is he? The reindeer, I mean."

"Secured in my van," Rob says. "I should probably go check on him if you don't need me..."

"Meredith?" I'd recognize Jeremy's voice pretty much anywhere and I look over to see him remonstrating with the uniformed police officer standing guard at the entrance to the Hot Chocolate Hut. That's when I realize how empty this place is. The scores of children and parents who were here drinking hot chocolate and enjoying the festive atmosphere are gone, but then I don't suppose there's much point in waiting around to see Santa when Santa is... I gulp, and realize Rob's still waiting for me to reply.

"I'm fine," I say, forcing myself to smile. "Thank you for the hot chocolate."

He winks and strolls off, and I make my way over to where Jeremy is getting extremely agitated about being prevented from coming inside.

"You don't understand! My friend - look, that's her. Meredith! Merry, are you alright? People are saying...well, the word is you found a..." He looks at me, white as a sheet, and I wonder why he looks more traumatized by the news than I feel about actually stumbling over Bill's dead body.

"Can he come in?" I ask the police officer politely. "We won't go out to the - crime scene." This time I manage to say it without cringing and the police officer frowns as if he's not that keen to disobey a direct order from his superior, but eyes Jeremy as if he also doesn't want to prolong their argument by refusing.

"Oh, alright." He stands aside and Jeremy lunges past him, pulling me into an embrace. "But you'll have to explain yourself to Officer Kelly."

"We will," I promise, while Jeremy squeezes the air out of my lungs. I teeter backward, steering him further into the hut and away from the irritated police officer while I wriggle out of my friend's strong arms. "Can you - not?" I manage, at last managing to get free. "I'm fine."

"But you very nearly weren't!" Jeremy exclaims, stepping back to survey me carefully. "Are you sure you're ok?"

"I'll be better when they find whoever did this," I say, taking a sip of my drink before my hands have time to shake again. The two issues - 1, that Bill/Santa was murdered a few feet from where we're still standing, and 2, that someone unknown is responsible for that murder - don't fail to make me shudder.

"Meredith."

Officer Kelly - or as I know her, Kate - strides out of the grotto and into the hut, with a deep frown creasing her forehead. When she spots Jeremy, her frown deepens.

"What are you doing here? Nobody was supposed to be allowed in here. Especially nobody who wasn't here when..."

Jeremy is grinning at her, and she rolls her eyes.

"Never mind." She turns to me, laying a light hand on my arm. "How are you doing?"

"Ok." I take another sip of my hot chocolate and realize I've drunk almost the whole thing. "Better."

"Good." Kate smiles, but it's not her usual smile. This is her *just-business* smile, and I know what's coming before she even says it. "I'm going to need to take a statement from you. Let's go sit..." She scans the room, wincing when she catches sight of the teenaged elves who are now clinging to each other and still, somehow, sobbing. I'm amazed they have any tears left. "Let's sit over there." She points to an empty table at the opposite end of the hut and steers me toward it. Jeremy follows us, pulling up a chair to sit next to me until Kate shoots him a withering look. "I only need to talk to Meredith."

"I'm here for moral support," Jeremy says, taking hold of my hand as soon as I let go of my now-empty hot chocolate mug. "Right, Merry?"

"Fine," I say, knowing that he's not about to walk away now. It's actually kind of nice, having him next to me, and I draw a little extra strength from his presence. From both of them, actually. If anyone had to interview me about a murder, I'm glad it's Kate. "So what do you need to know?"

"Just tell me whatever you remember."

"Well, I did already talk to..." I scan the room for the officious police officer who tried to keep Jeremy outside and point to him.

"Tell me," Kate says, smiling at me. "Just start at the beginning. You were working with Bill on Santa's grotto."

"Yes. I'd come out to get the camera from Nutella - from one of the teenagers." I don't want to admit I can only remember their elf names. "The little boy who was visiting Santa had a sister, so I scooped her up too so we could take the photo of both of them together." I look around and see both Matthew and his sister looking entirely unfazed at another table with two adults who must be their parents. Mom and Dad look more traumatized by the whole event than either of their children do.

"By the time I got back into the grotto, Matthew was on his own and Bill was nowhere to be seen. I knew there was a back door out of the grotto into the street which Bill showed me earlier, so I ducked out, thinking he was just taking a call or something. And then…" There's a lump in my throat and I try to swallow past it. "That's when I found him."

"Right." Kate is hurriedly tapping into her phone, making note of everything I say. "And was he…" She pauses, wrinkling her brow even further as she tries to think how to phrase her question.

"He was dead," I say flatly. "Bleeding from the head, actually." It sounds extra callous even to my ears, and I feel Jeremy wince beside me. I ignore him, fixing my gaze on Kate. "Did you find the murder weapon?"

"Not yet." Kate gets to her feet. "I'm going to go have another talk with the children - Matthew, did you say?" I nod, remembering I never did find out what his sister was called. She walks off and Jeremy turns to me, a wary smile on his face.

"So, I guess you won't have to be an elf anymore." His smile falters. "Always a silver lining."

"Look, I just need to speak to…yes, I realize this is a crime scene, but - Maggie! Hey, Maggie!"

Both Jeremy and I look over to the door, where the police officer on guard is trying to keep someone else out of the Hot Chocolate Hut. It's an older man and my stomach turns over as I recognize the red suit and big fake beard.

"Maggie!" He tries again to catch Maggie's attention, but the owner of the hut is sitting all alone, her eyes red-rimmed and teary, staring at nothing.

"Let me try and deal with this," I say to Jeremy, standing and making my way to the doorway.

"No more favors," the police officer says to me, shooting a dirty look over my shoulder to where Jeremy is still sitting. "This isn't a free-for-all, you know."

"I know." I turn to the impatient man dressed as Santa demanding to be allowed in. "What are you doing here?" I ask. I'm too tired to be polite, but then I think that maybe there's one person in all of Silver Brook who hasn't heard what's happened. "Oh, George. I'm sorry. You probably don't know. There's been a..." I stop myself before saying *murder* and change it to something slightly more palatable. "An accident."

"I know." George beams at me. "I guess there is a vacancy for someone to play Santa, after all!"

Chapter Six

My house has felt weirdly deserted ever since Neil left, but by the time I fall through the front door tonight, I'm kind of grateful for the quiet. Nobody is asking me questions. Nobody is tearfully clinging to me demanding comfort like *they're* the ones who stumbled over a dead body. And I can finally get out of this wretched elf costume! I strip as I go, leaving a trail of green and red all the way up my staircase, and head straight for the bathroom. Emerging thirty minutes later, after the longest, hottest shower known to man, I start to feel slightly more human again and I pad back downstairs in my comfiest pajamas, debating whether I can face cooking something healthy for dinner. I give it precisely one and a half minutes of considered thought before whipping out my phone and opening my local takeout delivery app. *There are things to love about being single,* I think, as I plop down on the sofa. *Nobody else to worry about. Nobody to judge my food choices.* My lips quirk as I build my order. *Nobody stealing half of my pad thai and calling it* sharing...

There's a knock at my door right before I hit submit on my order and I groan, planning to ignore it until the knock comes a second time, followed by a voice I recognize.

"I know you're home, Merry."

Kate Kelly might be Silver Brook's best police officer, but she's also my friend.

"I brought food."

Canceling my half-filled takeout order, I toss my phone onto the sofa and stand, crossing to the front door and opening it to let my friend in.

"Nice outfit," she says, with a grin, and I step aside, allowing her to step inside. She walks straight through to the kitchen and is already loading two plates before I can stop her.

"Pad thai?" She passes one plate to me.

"You read my mind." I smile. "Genuinely, I was just about to order."

"Then I saved you a job." Kate grabs her plate and ushers me towards the table. "Which means you owe me, and that's good because I...need a favor."

I feign outrage, even though I kind of saw this coming. I don't answer straight away, focusing on my meal, and Kate manages all of one mouthful before hurrying out a convoluted explanation.

"...so anyway, with Trainor out of town, I'm kind of in charge, and this is my first big case - the only big case, really, that's landed in Silver Brook in...well....in a long time. And I'm heading up the investigation. You were there, so...I was hoping...can you tell me everything you remember?"

"Didn't we already do this?" I arch one eyebrow, trying to make light of the fact that I don't want to revisit my memory of the murder scene I've just about managed to forget.

"No." Kate shakes her head, then nods. "Kind of. Yes. But this is something less formal. Off the record." Her lips quirk. "I need to know who else was there today. Who might be a suspect, or at least a person of interest."

I hesitate, but honestly, this has been exactly where my mind's been racing to all evening anyway, and I'd rather talk it over with my friend than think about it alone. I push my plate to one side and begin counting people out on my fingers.

"Well, there was me and Bill. He had two little kids in the grotto with him before we went missing."

"Matthew and Eleanor." Kate nods. "We can rule them out. Their parents, too. Alibis."

I roll my eyes, but then decide my friend is nothing if not thorough.

"Well, if it's a matter of alibis, you can rule out just about everyone on my list. The Hot Chocolate Hut was heaving with people, and everyone will have seen me and the other two elves running around trying to keep the kids in line."

"Right. You, Jessica and Ella." I frown and Kate smirks at me. "Your two elf friends."

"Oh, you mean Zany and Nutella." I nod, sagely. "We refer to each other by our elf names now."

"Good to know." Kate's grin turns sympathetic. "So I can rule out the kids and the elves, and there's no way Bill did this to himself. Who else was around today?"

"Who wasn't?" I shrug my shoulders. "Half the town comes out to visit the Christmas Market, you know that. And Maggie's is a favorite stop for hot chocolate." I frown, thinking that despite the crowds I hadn't seen her rushing about that morning. I shake my head. Just because I couldn't remember spotting her didn't mean she wasn't there. "So, Maggie..." I keep counting. "And oh! Rob was there."

Kate raises her eyebrows.

"Rob the reindeer guy." I remember how concerned he was about me right after my grim discovery and feel my cheeks redden. "Anyway, that's all the staff, unless you want to count the two grinches."

"Explain." Kate has opened an app on her phone and is noting down everything I say.

"It's probably nothing..." She's looking at me pointedly, so I continue. "Peter Stalker was not happy about our stall being set up right in front of his book shop. He got quite agitated, actually, and there was something else..." I frown, trying to remember exactly what he'd said that seemed strange at the time. "He made some comment about Bill being involved in raising funds for charity...hinting that he shouldn't be trusted with the money..." I shake my head. "He must have just been making it up, though, because Bill's been Silver Brook's go-to Santa for years. People would have noticed before now if he was up to something."

"Hmmm." Kate looks thoughtful but doesn't say any more on the subject. "And grinch number two?"

"Oh." I wince. "I probably shouldn't have called him a grinch, he's kind of the opposite. George Montgomery. He was complaining about being passed over to play Santa again this year. So much so that he'd turned up in his own handmade version of Santa's costume. He came back later, right after news broke about Bill, announcing he was on the spot and ready to take on the job, now that there was a vacancy."

"*Now there's a vacancy?*" Kate's incredulous. "He said that?"

"Pretty much." I take one last bite of my noodles. "He seemed kind of gleeful about it. But you don't think..." The food turns to ash in my mouth and I force myself to swallow. "He wouldn't...I mean, not just so he could play Santa...he's not a ..." I can't make my lips form the word. *Murderer.* There's a long silence and at last, Kate lets out a sigh.

"I don't know, but it's certainly worth having a chat with him." She taps her phone again and the screen goes black. "Thanks, Merry, that was helpful." She eyes my plate. "Want any more? That was only half the container. You know Mrs. Wu's portions."

"I'm good," I say. The food sits heavily in my stomach and I regret eating it now my thoughts have turned back to which of my neighbors might be a murderer. I think of Bill's empty, sightless eyes and remember the tearful figure of his wife when she arrived on the scene with one of Kate's colleagues. She'll be alone tonight, too. "I wonder if we should take something to Ivy."

"Rob - what did you call him? The *reindeer guy*? He said he'd stop in and check on her. She's due a visit from him, anyway."

"What?" I stifle a laugh, grateful for the way our conversation has switched from the macabre. "To address her reindeer needs?"

"You have no idea what Rob Castle does, do you?" Kate's eyes dance with amusement as she looks at me. "He's a vet, Merry. A pretty good one, actually. He brought my dog Bouncer back from the brink that time he snarfed those mushrooms before I could stop him, remember?"

Vaguely. I've never been a pet person, myself. Actually, no. *Neil* was never a pet person. I never really had the chance to figure out what I thought. I glance around the kitchen, wondering how different it would look with a kitty litter tray or a dog bed in one corner.

"Earth to Meredith!"

I straighten, turning to Kate, and realize she's been talking for a full minute while I entertained imaginary pet fantasies.

"Sorry."

"I asked if you were going to be alright here alone tonight. I can stay if you want company."

For a fleeting moment I'm tempted, but then I get hit with a wave of exhaustion and figure the only thing I'm going to do when Kate leaves is crawl into bed with a good book.

"I'm fine," I promise, smiling big in a gesture I hope is convincing. "Besides, I have to make sure my elf costume is clean and dry for tomorrow."

Kate's eyebrows lift.

"Maggie wants to continue with the grotto. It's for charity, after all, and why should the children of Silver Brook miss out on seeing Santa just because - because of what's happened?" I pause, an idea forming in my mind. "And anyway, you'll want me on the scene, won't you? I can be your eyes and ears on the ground!"

Kate opens her mouth to tell me no way, but I can see the very moment the light in her eyes changes. She's running this case, and she's desperate to solve it before her boss can come back and take all the credit. Having an eyewitness - and her best friend - right there on the scene might help her do it all the quicker.

"Fine. But don't do anything stupid."

"You're talking to a thirty-two-year-old woman voluntarily wearing a onesie in public. Define stupid?"

Chapter Seven

I wake up early the next day singing along to the pop song I have selected as my phone's alarm sound until a sense of dread stops me in my tracks.

Let me love you babyyyyy -

I'm confronted with an image of Bill's body, and blink it away, hurrying to get through my morning routine. As long as I keep moving, I'm not thinking too much about what happened yesterday or what might happen today. I volunteered to help Kate figure out who's responsible for Bill's murder because she's my friend, but the truth is if there's someone capable of killing Santa - or a guy dressed up to look like Santa - in my small, cozy home town then I want to know *who*. I'm halfway through my breakfast when I realize there was somebody else in Maggie's Hot Chocolate Hut yesterday that I forgot to mention to my friend. *Neil.*

"But I told him to go away," I say aloud, hearing my voice echo around my empty kitchen. "I told him to get lost, and he did." I don't remember seeing him after that one awkward interaction that morning. But what had he said when I'd asked him what he was doing there? *I'm here to see Santa.* I'd thought he was kidding, but maybe he hadn't been and I'd stumbled upon a murderer.

Neil? I shake my head, trying to get my imagination under control. My ex-husband is a lot of things I can't say out loud in front of a line of kids waiting to visit Santa's grotto, but he isn't and would never be a killer. My imagination is just running away with me, and I need to get it under control if I'm going to make any progress today.

Dressing in my elf costume feels strangely familiar this morning and I shove my jingle-bell shoes under my arm, ready to change into them once I get to the Hot Chocolate Hut. I slide my feet into my sneakers and grab my purse, deciding to park a bit away from the Christmas Market craziness and walk the rest of the way. I've got time, and I'm hoping that a little exercise might get my brain working. I need to be firing on all cylinders this morning if I'm going to check all of my colleagues' alibis and motives - and figure out what they're hiding. This last bit isn't under the remit of work Kate asked me to do, but it's my own addition and I think it's a useful one. Everybody's got secrets, haven't they? And some people might even kill to stop them from coming out. I stop short in front of Peter Stalker's bookstore, staring up into the huge gap where, just yesterday, the Hot Chocolate Hut had been standing. My gaze travels slightly to the right, and I see there's still a wigwam of police tape in place to keep people clear of the place where Bill's body lay, but other than that there's no indication anything even happened here. I shiver and wonder where the grotto has gone when Maggie's voice calls out to me from several feet away. I turn dumbly in her direction, and see she's standing right outside the newly-appointed hut looking just the same as ever only a little further down the high street. I walk towards her, clutching my elf shoes tightly and sliding a little on the frosty ground. *Careful there, Icey,* I remind myself, listening to the way my shoes jingle with every cautious step I take.

"We decided to move," she says, her voice thick. The smile she wears is pained, and I can see deep red circles around her eyes. She's really taken this whole thing hard, but then I guess she would, it happened right in her workplace. "Too many bad memories, and I don't want people thinking of what happened. People still want to be able to enjoy their hot chocolate and bring their kids to see - to see -" She trails off and I watch her sniff back more tears. "George has agreed to step into the breach and be our Santa, and I hate to say it, but he's really been great."

I'll bet he has! I remember my absurd thought last night that maybe he'd been desperate enough to get this gig he'd even kill for it. It seemed like nonsense, but now I can't help wondering.

"Come on, come in and get warmed up," Maggie says, patting me gently on the shoulder. "The other two girls are already here." She brightens. "I'm surprised anyone even turned up today, to be honest." She drops her voice. "I'm sure half of them are just curious. They'll be disappointed to see it's just business as usual." She swallows, noisily. "Or almost." She points me toward the grotto and I wave a greeting to Jessica and Ella. I don't feel right using their elf names anymore, and I'm determined to get to know them a little better. If I'm upset by Bill's death and the grand old age of thirty-two I can only imagine what the news has done to two teenagers.

"I'll go get my shoes on," I say, hurrying towards the grotto and stashing my bag and sneakers in one corner out of sight. Once my feet are back in their felt slippers and jingling with every step, I emerge from the grotto and go to join the two girls setting up fairy-lights along the makeshift path we've built for parents and children to queue along.

"Morning!" I say, hearing the false note of brightness in my voice and hoping it sounds more friendly than fake to my two young colleagues. Neither of them answers or looks at me and

I start to wonder if they've even noticed I'm there. It's a far cry from the way they both hung onto me yesterday afternoon, weeping and wailing about the tragedy of it all. I guess everything seems a little different in the cold light of day.

"So…" I try again. "Do you think we'll have many kids coming today?"

Ella shrugs but Jessica lifts her head, looking at me at last.

"My little brother's coming. He was so upset yesterday when he thought the grotto would be closed before he got the chance to come." She smiles, grimly. "We didn't tell him what happened."

"He'll find out," Ella says, grimly. "Nobody in this town can keep a secret." Her voice sounds kind of flat and I wonder if she's had friends hassling her for all the gory details. *A bit like my friend hassling me*, I think, remembering Kate's arrival. At least I got a free meal out of it.

"Hey, where's Fred Astaire?" I ask, finally noticing what's missing. There's no reindeer. *And no Rob*. I chase that thought away as quickly as it registers.

"Oh, Maggie decided not to have him back." Jessica smiles, sadly. "One less thing for us to worry about. He'll be back in Monroe Cove putting his feet up." She stifles a yawn. "Unlike us."

"Girls!" Maggie calls to us from the doorway. "Are you ready?"

"As we're ever going to be."

I sprint back to the grotto, leaving Ella and Jessica to welcome the first children. We'll switch in an hour and I decide I'll try and get a minute to speak to Ella. She seems so unlike herself I want to check there's nothing wrong. Bill's death seems to have hit her hard and I admit I'm a little worried about her.

"Ho ho h-oh." George's excitement drops when he sees I'm not a child. "Are there many waiting?"

"Quite a few," I say, grabbing a handful of candy canes and slipping the camera over my shoulder. "Ella and Jessica will send the first one any minute now."

"I thought you were Jessica," George says, vaguely.

There's a rustle by the doorway and we both plaster eager grins on our faces until the curtain parts and Kate steps through.

"Good morning!"

"This is supposed to be a *children's* grotto," George grumbles.

"And there are hundreds of them squirming to be let in just outside," she reassures him, before turning to catch my eye. My heart sinks and I steer her over to the corner of the room, where we can pretend we have a little privacy.

"What's wrong?" I ask, trying to read my friend's features for any clue.

"Nothing!" Kate pulls something out of her pocket and holds it out to me. "I was just on my way to work and realized I forgot to give you this last night." She winks at me. "Nutella Jollysocks! Can't have you turning up without a name badge!" She glances at her phone. "I'd better run. I'll stop by later, though. And remember - don't do anything stupid."

"Right." I grin and wave her off, before finding my place next to Santa ready to greet his first visitor of the day. It's then that I turn the name badge over in my hand and squint at it, confused. *Nutella Jollysocks?* Kate said she'd found it next to Bill's body, which might make sense if I'd dropped it when I tripped over him. But if I'd dropped my badge, it would have said *Icey Sprinkelcakes.* My gaze strays toward the doorway and I imagine the two elves standing just outside it. What had Ella's elf-name badge been doing there?

Chapter Eight

"...and a very merry Christmas to you, young man!" George lets out another jolly *ho-ho-ho* and high-fives his little visitor, and I hand the boy his candy cane and a paper ticket to come back and collect his photograph at the end of the day. As soon as he leaves the grotto, George pulls his fake fluffy beard off his face and sighs. "Is that the last one?"

"For now." I peer out into the Hot Chocolate Hut and see Jessica and Ella have put the *back in five minutes* sign at the head of the queue. "Time for a break, and I'm going to go get a drink. Do you want anything?"

"Not for me, dear." George salutes me with a water bottle. "I came prepared!"

My smile freezes a little and I stop on my way out of the grotto, turning to look back at George. He doesn't *look* like a murderer...but he's certainly pleased to be in this role he never would have got if Bill hadn't been killed.

"You seem to be enjoying yourself," I say, striving to keep my tone light. "Have you played Santa before?"

"Not officially." George takes another swig of his water and shakes his head. "It always went to Bill..." He trails off and when I squint I think I see tears in George's eyes.

"You know each other well?"

"Yes..." George blinks rapidly a few times, then looks back at me. "We hated each other for over a decade." My surprise at this easy admission must be obvious because he quickly explains himself. "We used to work together, and when there was a chance for a promotion, only one of us could get the role. I needed that job. I deserved it, too, with all the extra hours I'd been putting in." His hand clamps tightly around his water bottle and I hold my breath, scared that if I make a single sound to distract him he'll stop telling this story. "I spent ages working on a proposal that I knew would clinch it for me. Got the whole thing printed professionally, too. It looked beautiful. Anyway, I took it into work one morning, ready to make a presentation to the bosses only to discover Bill had beaten me to it." He scowls. "He'd got wind of what I was doing, and because he was all pally with the printers - like he is with everyone in this town - they'd let him have a peek at my proposal. Of course, he stole the whole thing and marched into the office an hour earlier, presenting it as *his* work."

My mouth falls open. This doesn't sound like Bill at all. It's so...awful!

"He got the promotion, of course. He always gets everything he wants." George's expression turns into a grim smile. "Well, not anymore, I guess..." He seems to remember I'm standing there, and his smile vanishes. "You must think I sound dreadful, talking like this. Especially about a man who's just died."

I shake my head, willing my features to remain neutral. Inwardly I'm screaming to go call Kate, but my feet remain rooted to the spot.

"The thing is, despite popular opinion, Bill was not a nice man. I guess I'm not the only one who thought so." He raised his water bottle. "Well, so long, Bill. I hope you're in a better place...but I doubt it."

I turn and stride away as quickly as my little elf legs will take me, trying to memorize all that George just said. If only I'd thought to record him! I fumble with my phone, wondering if I can go back and persuade him to repeat it while I covertly point my microphone toward him…but no. That'd be…what do they call it? Entrapment?

"Here you go, love!" Maggie passes me a steaming cup of hot chocolate without me even having to ask. "Oh, Meredith! Are you alright? You look a bit pale. Here, sit down and have a proper rest. I'm going to ask one of those teenagers to take your place when you guys open up again. It isn't right they just stand around chatting to their friends and leave you to do all the work." She frowns. "And sneaking off all the time to meet their boyfriends. It's just not good enough."

"What?"

"I'm surprised you didn't notice! There's almost always one of them disappearing off for an unscheduled break."

Without meaning to, I turn my head to look at the two teenagers, both blonde heads bent over their phones. Ella's name badge is still poking me uncomfortably in my pocket and I realize I haven't had the chance to give it back to her yet.

"What's wrong?" Maggie is looking at me, her wry smile fading.

"Nothing." I take a sip of my coffee and smile at her. "Just grateful to take a break."

"Go put your feet up." She points me to an empty table and I do as she suggests, propping my feet up on the chair next to me.

"You know, I do love those shoes."

I hear the smile in Jeremy's voice before I see him, approaching with a takeaway cup from a popular coffee chain in his hand.

"Don't let Maggie see you drinking out of that," I warn, as he sits down next to me. He wraps his big hands around the cup, obscuring the logo, and winks at me.

"So, how's your day?" He takes a covert sip of his coffee but despite his feigned ease, I can tell he's watching me closely.

"Did Kate send you to check up on me?"

"She emphatically did *not*."

Kate and Jeremy have been in the most convoluted on-again-off-again relationship in the world for about as long as I've known them. They're currently off-again, although that doesn't mean much, and I'm pretty sure they're in near-daily contact talking about me anyway, even before this whole Bill murder thing.

"Right." I raise my eyebrows at him over the rim of my mug and take another sip of my hot chocolate. "So, you're here because...?"

"I want to see Santa?" He looks so earnest that I laugh, choking on my mouthful of hot chocolate. After a lot of coughing and spluttering and a slap on my back that was a lot harder than it needed to be - thanks a lot, Jeremy - I'm finally able to speak again. Something about his comment jars with me and it's not just the absurd notion of my best guy-friend coming to visit the jolly red elf.

"What?" It's Jeremy's turn to stare at me, now, and his brows knit in concern. "Why are you looking at me like that?"

"You just reminded me of someone..." I frown, turning Jeremy's comment over in my head. *I want to see Santa.* Where did I hear that recently?

"Tom Cruise?" Jeremy jokes, striking a pose I think is meant to make him look like a movie star. "Brad Pitt?"

"Neil!"

"Thank you, *no*." Jeremy's face transforms into a look of disgust and I shake my head, trying to explain but struggling to keep up with my racing thoughts.

"Neil said that - yesterday - he said he wanted to see Santa. That's odd, don't you think? Because then, a little later..." I trail off, and Jeremy takes a full minute to react.

"You think *Neil* had something to do with this? With Bill's death?"

I shrug my shoulders, and the motion make's Ella's pin badge poke painfully into my hip.

"I don't know what to think," I say, honestly. "But it's odd that he was even here."

Jeremy's face settles back into the frown he usually wears when the topic of my soon-to-be-officially-ex husband comes up.

"Not that odd." He folds his arm, leaving his coffee cup on the table. "You were here, after all."

"He doesn't care about me," I say, waving him off.

"He cares about -"

"Jeremy Walton!"

Maggie's screech is enough to make the volume of conversation in the hut drop by several decibels as she storms over to our table, her hand outstretched in horror.

"What is that?"

Jeremy's quicker than me to realize she's pointing at his traitorous coffee cup and he sweeps it swiftly into the trash can where it belongs.

"Nothing." He shoots one of his million-dollar smiles her way and it works like it always does. "But I wonder how long

I'm going to have to wait until you bring me a proper drink, Maggie!"

I groan, lifting my mug to my lips but I don't take another sip. Instead, I'm thinking hard. I need to figure out what Neil was really doing here. And if the two teenagers were running here there and everywhere yesterday then maybe - just maybe - they had more to do with this than I thought. My gaze strays to where they're standing and I realize Ella's gone. I leap to my feet, so swiftly I spill hot chocolate on my sleeve. Dabbing at the spot, I put my cup down on the table and turn a slow circle, scanning the hut for any sign of her.

"Going somewhere?" Jeremy asks, watching my pantomime with amusement.

"I'll be right back," I promise, digging into my pocket and pulling out Ella's badge. This is my chance to find out just what she was doing when she lost it yesterday. My features settle into a grim smile as I duck back through the grotto and out the back door, ignoring George's cheerful salutation. *I just need to find her first.*

Chapter Nine

This section of Silver Brook's Main Street is a lot less frenetic than where we had the Hot Chocolate Hut set up yesterday, so I easily spot Ella talking to a tall, dark-haired boy. *Talking* is putting it politely, and I clear my throat loudly as I approach.

"What?" Ella breaks away and turns to look at me. I'm surprised to see she's been crying.

"You dropped this," I say, holding out the pin badge. She stares at it a moment before taking and pinning it swiftly to her elf costume.

"Thanks." She turns back to her boyfriend, who's taken a decorous step away from her, but is still holding her warmly by the hand. "You'd better go."

"Are you sure?" His voice is low, but even I can hear the affection in it. My heart turns over. It's a long time since a guy looked at me that lovingly. "I can stick around."

"It's fine," Ella says, sharply, then smiles at him. "I'm ok. I'll call you later."

He presses a kiss to the top of her head, then slopes off, leaving us two elves standing there in awkward silence.

"He seems nice," I say, awkwardly. "Have you been seeing each other long?"

"A while." Ella's distracted, her gaze darting this way and that and I rush to reassure her that she's not in any trouble. Not with me, anyway.

"It's nice that you're able to squeeze in a few minutes together, what with everything being so busy this week." She glares at me, and I keep rambling on. "I mean, it's not like *I* have anyone worth sneaking out of work to see." I grin, trying to keep my voice natural and failing miserably. "Is that where you were yesterday? When you lost your badge, I mean?"

Ella's face crumples, and to my surprise she reaches for me. I almost buckle under her weight but manage to stay standing, patting her awkwardly on the shoulder.

"It's ok...shhh...it's ok."

"It's *not* ok!" She wrenches free of me and staggers a few paces back toward the grotto before turning to look back in my direction. "Sorry." She sniffs back the rest of her tears and tries to regain her composure. "I just...I mean...." She sighs, wiping her nose on the sleeve of her elf costume. "I suppose I might as well tell you. It'll be common knowledge before long." She takes in a shaky, juddering breath. "I didn't sneak out to see Adam yesterday. I snuck out to see Bill."

"Bill?" My stomach turns over. He's old enough to be her father - her *grand*father! My shock must show on my face because she rolls her eyes.

"Ew, not like that. He - he's my...my....dad." The last voice comes so quietly that I'm not sure I hear her right. I lean a little closer, my eyes wide, and fixed on her.

"Bill Barraclough was your father?"

Ella nods, miserably.

"He and my Mom had an affair sixteen years ago, and..." She makes a mocking jazz-hands pose and grimaces at me. "She only just told me. *Merry Christmas, Ella, here's your real dad's name...*" She shakes her head, slowly. "It's why I took this job, to get to know him, you know? I thought..." She shrugs her thin shoulders. "I don't know what I thought. But he - he wasn't interested." Her eyes grow steely. "No, he was angry. He made me promise not to tell anyone and got really mad that Mom had even told me, like I don't have a right to know who my real father is." She shakes her head. "It's not like I want anything from him. I have a great stepdad. I'm fine. But I just...I wanted to get to know him. And he didn't want anything to do with me."

There's something so small and sad about her that I reach out, pulling her into a hug I'm not sure she wants but she certainly needs. *So Ella confronted Bill about her past and he rebuffed her. That's certainly something that might make her angry as well as sad. But angry enough to...* I tense and lean away, pointing her back towards the grotto.

"I can cover for you, if you'd rather not work today," I say, softly. I take a quick, appraising glance at her and try to work out if someone as small and slight as she is could possibly find the strength to bludgeon a man to death. I blink. This is absurd, and I shake my head, trying to clear the images that my imagination is conjuring.

"No, it's fine." She sniffs, wiping away the congealed mascara that's pooled beneath her eyes. "I'm not going to let this ruin my life. He almost ruined Mom's, but she came through it all alright." She smiles, and I'm amazed at her strength. "Forgive and forget, right?" Her smile grows wry. "Or *forget*, at least."

Jeremy appears around the side of the hut, looking relieved when he spots me.

"Oh, thank goodness. You'd...ah...you'd better hurry back. Maggie's disappeared and your other little elf friend is not coping very well with all the kids wanting to see Santa..."

Ella nods and hurries into the grotto, leaving me alone with Jeremy, who's looking at me with concern.

"Are you alright?"

"Fine," I tell him, but my mind is turning cartwheels. Bill Barraclough is Ella's *dad*? He had an affair sixteen years ago and managed to keep the fact that it produced a whole child a secret.

He has secrets. That's what George had said when he first ranted about the unfairness of Bill Barraclough being Silver Brook's beloved Santa Clause every year. He wasn't kidding. *I wonder what else Bill was hiding...and if it was something that got him killed.*

"Come on, we'd better get back."

"*You'd* better get back." Jeremy winks at me. "I'm a free agent today, and now I've checked up on you -" He catches himself too late and hangs his head.

"You just wanted to see Santa, huh?" I'm glaring at him, but I'm not mad. It's quite touching that Jeremy and Kate can overcome their animosity long enough to keep an eye on me. "What did Kate say?"

"Nothing!" he insists. "Well, not much." He sighs. "She said you were going to do some sleuthing and that, knowing you, it might end up getting you in trouble." He grins at me. "But you're fine! Look at you! No trouble, no nothing!" His grin fades. "Right?"

"Right." I decide now is not the time to tell him about Bill's secret child, or the fact that plenty of people seem not to have been his biggest fan. I'm more eager to get back to work, keep my ear to the ground, and hopefully find out something else useful I can present to Kate later, to justify my sleuthing and prove that it was worth me risking getting in so-called trouble. "And now I'm going to go back and spread a little more Christmas cheer if you've quite finished checking up on me." I flounce off but pause to wave at him from the door to the grotto so he knows I'm not really mad. Christmas isn't the time for holding grudges.

"Merry!"

Except in certain cases.

"Neil." I don't even bother trying to smile at my ex-husband, who's standing adjacent to the queue of children eager to see Santa. I glance at Ella, but she seems a bit more like her old self and is happily chatting with the little girl at the front of the line, who is telling her all about the pony she's about to demand from Santa just as soon as we let her into the grotto. My gaze flicks back to Neil. "What are you doing here?" I hold up a hand. "And *don't* say you're here to see Santa. You are too old and too ugly to pull that off."

"Ouch!" He grins and reaches into his back pocket, pulling out his wallet which appears to be bulging with ready cash. "Maybe I'll think twice about giving you this, then?" He proceeds to count out a pile of notes he holds out to me and I'm so shocked it takes me a minute to react. "What are you doing?"

"Hey, Mister!" A little boy calls. "Are you giving out money?"

"Give me that!" I snatch the cash off him and squint down at it, certain this is some kind of elaborate - and strange - joke. "Where did you get this?"

"That's not important." He slides his significantly lighter wallet back into his pocket and smiles at me. "I felt kind of bad for leaving you with all our bills after..." He clears his throat, and I notice how he's trying hard not to mention the Shelly-sized elephant in the room. "Anyway, consider this a goodwill gesture. My contribution. Something to make things a little easier for you."

"Easier for me?" I repeat, dumbly. Part of me wants to throw the money back in his face because after the amount of heartache and stress he's caused me a few dollars are the least of my concerns, but I can't help but total up the amount and think how many zeros this handful of cash is going to wipe off my debt total. *Merry Christmas, Meredith.* "Well." I straighten and slide the money into the pocket of my onesie. "It's the least you could do."

Neil nods, having the grace to look a little chagrined. I start to feel like maybe - just maybe - there's a way for us to be friends after all this is resolved, but then he has to go and ruin it by opening his mouth. *As usual.*

"So, those papers..."

My stomach clenches. That's what this is all about. He isn't trying to help me or cover some of the bills he'd left me scrambling to pay. This is a bribe. I fold my arms and glare up at him, daring him to keep talking.

"It's just, the lawyers are getting ready to take off work for the Christmas break, and it'd get everything moving a little quicker if we could both submit our packets sooner rather than later...and..." His voice drops to a whisper. "Shelly and I..."

"I'm sure I don't want to do anything that might make life a little harder for *Shelly and you,*" I mimic, in a low whisper. "But in case you have noticed, I'm a little busy right now." I stride back to join Ella at the head of the queue, dismissing Neil with a toss of my head. "So, I guess you'll just have to wait for me to sign and return our divorce papers when I'm good and ready."

It's a petty victory. Not even a victory because I'm cheating myself out of a settlement just as much as I'm punishing Neil with every day I delay returning them. But just then it's about the only card I have to hold over him, and I'm darn well going to enjoy it. Season of goodwill or not.

An idea occurs to me and I turn back to Neil just as he's getting ready to leave.

"Is that what you were coming to see me about yesterday? The papers? The -" I stop myself from saying *bribe*. "Money?"

Neil hesitates, then nods.

"That was part of it. I needed to talk to Bill, but...yeah."

I want to see Santa. My skin crawls.

"What about?"

"Huh?"

"What did you need to talk to Bill about? I mean, it could be kind of important now, don't you think? Kate's still trying to build a picture of what happened, and..."

"I didn't kill him!" There's an anxious note to Neil's words and his voice is just that bit too loud to avoid carrying to the eager, inquisitive ears of the waiting children. Ella glares at us, and I shoot her an apologetic look. Neil takes me by the arm and pulls me a few steps away, just enough that we can whisper without being overheard. "Look, he owed me some money, if you really must know." He rakes a hand through his hair, and the gesture is so familiar it makes my heart hurt. I swallow past a lump in my throat.

"He owed you money? For what?"

"A bet." Neil smiles, crookedly, and I realize he's still exactly the same as he ever was. He'd always loved the thrill of betting on local sports teams - never a lot, and it wasn't ever anything problematic, but a "harmless flutter" had been one of the chief joys of his life. Especially when he won. The money I have stashed in my pocket burns against my hip.

"That's where this came from? Betting with Bill Barraclough?"

"No!" Neil is indignant. "Not only Bill. There's a few of us." He can tell that isn't having the effect he thought it would and lets out a sigh. "Look, it's just a few hands of poker, ok? Me, Bill, a few others." He at last has the grace to look a little sorry. "I guess we'll need to find someone else now to take Bill's place, although he was such a sore loser..."

I'm staring at him now without blinking, sifting various pieces of the puzzle in my mind. Bill has secrets...Bill can't be trusted around money...Bill has a long-standing seat at a poker game with a few other guys in town... I grab Neil tight by the forearm.

"Who else plays?"

"What? Why? Just a few guys...nobody you'd know." He shakes me off. "Why are you making such a big deal about this? Shelly doesn't care what I do in my own time..."

"Good for Shelly," I say, through clenched teeth. "But I need to know who else has a seat at that game. Because somebody killed Bill Barraclough, Neil, or have you forgotten that? And maybe you weren't the only person he owed money to."

Chapter Ten

"Jessie! Jessie!! Is he here?"

A little boy in a big red hat runs at me, altering his course at the last moment to tackle Jessica, who is standing next to me counting the kids along the line waiting to see Santa.

"He's here," she promises him, wriggling free of his grip. "Now go get in line and wait with all the other boys and girls." The little boy lets out a theatrical sigh but does as she suggests and she shoots me a look. "My little brother." She grins. "I think he was hoping I'd sneak him in ahead of everybody else, but I told him he'd have to wait."

"What a mean big sister!" I say, surprised to find I'm quite enjoying getting to know the two teenagers that were so infuriating to me yesterday. After Ella's big confession, I've felt a sort of maternal urge to keep an eye on her, and I realize that in her own way that's exactly what Jessica has been doing too, distracting her with gossip and sticking to her like glue to keep her from getting too morose about Bill.

Jessica grins at me and waves the next child into the grotto. I'm still smiling when a familiar voice reaches me.

"Well, you look a lot better than the last time I saw you!"

Rob Castle drops the little girl he's holding onto her own two feet and straightens, smiling at me. My knees wobble and I force myself to remain upright, running a quick calculation to figure out how long it is until we get a break. I must be light-headed from lack of food. It's not like Rob is *that* good-looking...

"Who's this?" Jessica asks, bending down to smile at the little girl, who unbuttons her coat and introduces herself.

"Jessica."

"Great name!" Big Jessica high-fives her, and now that I'm a little more in control of my faculties I smile at Rob.

"Your daughter?"

"My niece." He rakes a hand through his short, wavy hair and leans a little closer to me. I try to ignore the heady cedar scent of his cologne. "I'm entertaining her while her folks do a little last-minute shopping." He straightens, looking down at the little girl. "So, we thought we'd come to see Santa, didn't we? Now, go find the back of the queue, Jess. I'll come join you in a second, I just want to talk to my friends real quick."

She beams and dashes off, and in a moment I see her chatting happily with Jessica's little brother, both bouncing on the soles of their little feet in excitement to see Santa Clause. My heart lifts. I'm glad, now, that Maggie decided we should keep going with Santa's grotto, even after everything awful happened with Bill. It would be a shame for these children to miss out.

"So, are you ok?"

Rob's talking to me and I'm surprised to see what looks like a genuine concern in his green eyes. I remember how gently he handed me a mug of hot chocolate after I discovered Bill's body and feel a tiny thrill go through me.

"Fine," I tell him, squaring my shoulders and trying to convey that I'm not the type of woman who falls apart over something like a little murder. "Keeping busy."

"I see that." He raises his eyebrows at the queue of children and lets out a surprised little exhalation. "Maybe I should have brought Fred Astaire back! I didn't think so many children would want to come."

"Well, we aren't exactly advertising what happened," I say, softly. I remember something Kate told me and turn to him. "How is Mrs. Barraclough doing?"

He looks surprised, then shrugs his broad shoulders.

"About as well as can be expected. Snuffy is doing a lot better, so that's been something." He winces. "Not that I'm trying to say a sick cat compares to losing her husband." He shakes his head. "Forget it. I'm rambling. Mostly because I wanted an excuse to keep talking to you." He looks past me to Jessica, who's lurking a bit too close for someone who's pretending so hard not to be listening to us. "To both of you."

"We're fine," I say, a little hurt that he isn't interested in me after all. "We're -"

"Hey, Mister!"

Both Rob and I turn at the sound of a small voice and smile as a little boy marches up to confront us. My smile is bigger: I recognize this particular little boy, who pauses to push his glasses further up his tiny nose.

"Good morning, Matthew!" I smile down at him, looking for his sister and certain that if he's here, so will she be, somewhere. "What are you doing here again?"

He lets out a sigh more suited to a man ten times his age.

"Mommy and Daddy brought us. They said they ought to so that we don't get traumatized."

"That's a big word!" Rob points out, fighting a laugh.

"S'what they said." Matthew shrugs his shoulders. "But why don't you have your reindeer with you?" He looks a little disappointed. "Is he alright?"

"He's just fine," Rob reassures him. "He's happily at home enjoying an extra few days off. You want to see?" He pulls out his phone and tabs through a few photos until he finds the one he's looking for. I subtly peer over his shoulder and see Fred Astaire's regal nose poking out of a red-and-white painted stable.

"Is that his house?" Matthew asks, fascinated. I watch as Rob explains a little about where the reindeer lives and what he gets up to on the daily and feel a stray smile creep onto my face. He's so good with kids. I feel eyes on me and when I see the knowing look Jessica is shooting me I hurry to rearrange my features into something neutral.

"You'd better go get in the queue," I tell Mathew. "If you're here to see Santa, I mean."

"No, that's ok." He hands Rob's phone back to him and looks up at me and I can see another volley of detailed questions brewing in his tiny mind. "Who were you talking about just now? Mrs Barra…Barra…" He's struggling with the name, and I fill it in for him.

"Mrs. Barraclough?"

He nods.

"Well, she's…"

"She's Santa's wife," Rob puts in. "The Santa from yesterday. The one who…" He trails off, looking at me and I shake my head, desperately. I've got no idea what Matthew's parents have said to him about Bill's murder, but I'm pretty sure their idea of bringing him back here didn't involve traumatizing him further by talking about the nearest and dearest of the deceased.

"She's not." Matthew shakes his head, looking at us like we're trying to trick him. I remember his assertion the previous day and lay a hand on Rob's arm, stopping him from answering.

"I mean, she's Santa's helper's wife." I smile like me and Matthew are both in on a secret.

"No." Matthew shakes his head. "Santa's wife's over there." He turns and points towards Maggie, who is weaving her way through tables filled with happy Hot Chocolate Hut customers. "I saw them together yesterday." He screws up his face in a grimace. "*Kissing.*"

I open my mouth to contradict him, sure he's confused, but his mom calls him to come and join her and Eleanor at the back of the queue, so he hurries off before I can say a word.

"Weird kid," Rob remarks, with a chuckle.

"Confused kid." I shake my head. Maggie's not all that fond of George and she certainly wasn't Bill's wife. I'd met Mrs. Barraclough, and from what Kate said, she'd been at home all day yesterday - barring that first fight I'd accidentally witnessed. Another thought assails me and I feel my blood run cold in my veins. Bill may have had a wife, but he'd also had a mistress - one sixteen years ago that resulted in a baby that he'd successfully managed to keep secret from pretty much everyone in the small, nosy town of Silver Brook. What if Ella's mom wasn't the only woman he'd had an affair with? What if Maggie...

"Oops, I'd better run." Rob's already walking away when I look up, and I see him scoop a tearful little Jessie into his arms and whisper something comforting in her ear that turns her sniffles into smiles. I can feel myself smiling at the image and shake my head. This isn't the time to get distracted by Rob Castle, however cute he looks cradling his adorable niece like that. I'm about to make a discovery, I can feel it, if only I can let my brain make the connections it's trying to make.

"You can manage here for a moment, can't you?" I ask Jessica, but I'm already walking away before she has a chance to answer. I'm headed straight for Maggie, but someone else reaches her before I'm able to, and I'm so stunned by the woman I see that it stops me dead in my tracks.

"Mrs. Barraclough!"

"Meredith!" Maggie turns towards me with a smile so bright it's bordering on desperation. "You remember Ivy?"

"Of course she does." The plump, round-faced woman turns to me and squeezes my arm. "You're the poor young lady who found him, aren't you?" Nobody needs to clarify who *him* is.

"How are you doing, Ivy?" I ask, my voice thin. What I want to ask is *what are you doing here?* But I can't bring myself to do anything but smile at her with that same pitying smile that people gave me when they heard about Neil. *It must be a million times more unbearable when it's because of a death and not a divorce.* "Here, why don't you sit down? I'm sure Maggie will bring you a hot chocolate, and I -"

"Aren't you sweet!" Ivy shakes her head. "No, no. I don't need anything. I just wanted to come down here and wish you all a Merry Christmas, and to - to put my donation in the basket for the children's hospital." She pulls out her purse and starts rifling through her coins. Maggie meets my gaze, wearing the same slightly stunned expression I'm sure is plastered onto my face too. Of all the things a widow might want to do the day after her husband dies, this didn't seem to be one of them.

"How did you get here, Mrs. Barra - Ivy?" I ask when she counts out some change and hands it to me carefully. "Is someone with you?"

"No, no. It's just me." She smiles sadly, and as I see the tears well up behind her eyes I kick myself for being so foolish. *Way to remind her of everything she's just lost, Meredith!* "I parked my car and I thought I'd take a little walk down the high street and admire the Christmas lights. They do look very festive this year, don't you think?" She draws a shaky breath. "And I thought I couldn't avoid this place just because - because of what happened. I wanted to come and do my bit." She folds my fingers around the money she places into my palm. "And now I have!"

"Merry Christmas!" I blurt because I can't think of anything else to say.

"And to you, dear." She peers past me and makes a tutting sound. "Oh, dear. It looks like that other young elf might need some assistance."

I turn and see Jessica struggling to keep two very determined children from entering the grotto at once and I bid Mrs. Barraclough a swift goodbye before dashing over to help and dropping her donation in the fundraising bucket as I pass it. When order is restored I look back over my shoulder, but Bill's widow is nowhere to be seen. Maggie is still there, though, and she waves to get my attention.

"I just need to run down the street to the Jitterbug and change some cash. Can you two keep an eye on the hut as well as the grotto?"

I look at Jessica and she nods, immediately walking over to take charge of the quieter half of the room and leaving me to wrangle the children single-handedly. I fight a sigh. I guess I deserve that for ditching her not once but twice today.

"Alrighty." I clap my hands and turn back to the queue of eager littles. "Who's next?"

"Meeee!"

It's Jessie, who drags Rob eagerly forward, and he salutes me, laughing, as he follows his niece into the grotto, ducking his head so he can pass through the narrow door. I'm still smiling when I hear the loud rev of an engine outside the hut, followed by the squeal of brakes and a dull, sickening thud.

Chapter Eleven

"I just didn't see her! I mean, she came out of absolutely nowhere, and my car was already moving! When I hit that ice, I -"

"Shhh," I say soothingly to Ivy Barraclough. We're both sitting in the corridor of the small Silver Brook hospital, and she has a gauze patch taped over a small cut on her forehead. Maggie, it seems, wasn't so lucky.

The door to Maggie's hospital room opens and a capable-looking woman in hospital scrubs bustles out, looking at us with a vague frown.

"We're friends of Maggie's," I say before she can question us. "Is she going to be ok?"

"She's going to be fine." The doctor says, making a note or two in the chart she's holding. "But I'm not prepared to say anything more than that unless either of you is a family member." She raises her eyebrows, looking at us expectantly and both Ivy and I are forced to shake our heads. "Well, then you can content yourself in the knowledge that she's going to be fine." She looks at Ivy and compassion sweeps over her. "Just some bumps and bruises. Were you the driver?"

Ivy reaches up to press her fingertips against the thick gauze on her forehead and nods. She still looks as pale and anxious as she was when she climbed out of her car and saw Maggie lying on the street in front of her. I'd come running out of the hut to see what was the matter, and in the end I was the only one able to quickly bring Ivy to the hospital, following Maggie's ambulance in my car.

The doctor walks over and takes Ivy by the hand, smiling compassionately at her.

"Don't worry. Everyone knows it was an accident. With that ice on the ground…" She shudders. "It's just a miracle that you were both relatively unharmed." Her gaze flickers to me with a silent question.

"I just happened to be close by at the time," I say, gesturing to my elf costume with a grimace. "Working."

"Well, maybe you can take Mrs…"

"Barraclough," I volunteer when Ivy remains silent and tearful.

"Maybe you can take Mrs. Barraclough home. I will tell Maggie you came to see her, but she is resting now and won't be up to having visitors for some time yet." She smiles again and lets go of Ivy's hand, before marching down the corridor to the nurses' station to continue with her day.

Meekly, Ivy allows me to steer her back out to the parking lot and we make the journey home in near silence. She directs me to pull up outside a pretty cottage but doesn't immediately get out of the car.

"Won't you come in and have a cup of tea?" she asks at last, and I can tell from the rigid way she holds her head that she's really asking for company. I remember how cold and empty my house felt after Neil left and with everything this poor woman has been through in the last few days I can't say no. I peer into the back seat and reach for a sweater I pull on over my elf costume, and together we walk up the path to Ivy's house.

"Take a seat," she instructs me, pointing me to her living room, which is filled with the same over-stuffed suite my parents have in their lounge. The sight makes me feel instantly at home

- and exhausted! I step into the room, stifling a yawn, and pause to admire the framed photographs that line one wall. My heart sinks when I see Bill and Ivy together in all of them. Bill and Ivy on their wedding day. Bill and Ivy standing under a palm tree on some exotic vacation. Bill and Ivy...Bill and Ivy...Bill and Ivy. *And no children*, I think, recalling Ella with a shiver. Did Ivy even know about her? Would it hurt her to know her husband had a child out there somewhere that he hadn't wanted anything to do with for the whole sixteen years she'd been alive?

Every stray surface is covered with ornaments, some of them Christmassy but many not. I spy decorative china houses and one large trophy with engraving on it that I squint to read. *Silver Brook's Man of the Year, Bill Barraclough*. It's dated last year.

There's a huge Christmas tree in one corner of the room, cheerily decorated with color-co-ordinated ornaments and warm white lights twinkling merrily. I can't help but feel a little sorry for Ivy Barraclough, widowed so close to Christmas. At least I had some warning that my holiday season wasn't going to be like all the ones I'd had before. I wrench my gaze away from the tree, finding it just as painful as Ivy's photographs, and as I hear her moving around in the kitchen I decide to clear some space for her to put down our drinks. I turn to a small end table between two comfortable chairs and lift the pile of papers sitting on top of it. I don't mean to look at them, but as I'm searching for somewhere to safely stow them my gaze rests on the front page, and something familiar strikes me. These are just like the papers *I* keep moving around *my* living room, putting off dealing with them until the last possible moment. I'm reading before I'm even fully aware that I'm reading and the blood rushes in my ears. *Ivy and Bill were getting a divorce!* Or they would have been if she'd signed the papers. I flip to the back and see Bill's untidy scrawl dated a week ago.

"What are you doing?"

My head whips up, guiltily, but it's too late. Ivy is standing in the living room doorway, a steaming cup of tea in each hand, and there's a strange gleam in the eyes she is fixing on me.

"I'm sorry," I stammer, shoving the papers onto the bookshelf beside me. "I didn't mean to - I was just clearing - "

Ivy sighs, crossing the room towards me and putting our cups of tea down on the table I'd emptied.

"I guess now you know, there's no point in me playing the grieving widow anymore." When she looks up at me, her kind smile and sad eyes are gone. In its place is an expression I can't quite make sense of until she speaks again. "I hated what that man did to me. I just can't believe it took me this long to make him pay."

Chapter Twelve

I try to move but I'm not quick enough. Ivy grabs me by the elbow, her fingers digging into my arm.

"I would have got *her* too, if only you hadn't rushed onto the scene." She smiles, maniacally. "Not that I meant to. I was going to live and let live. She isn't the first woman to be taken in by Bill's charms and she probably wouldn't have been the last." Her smile fades and her gaze is fixed, unseeing, on some point in the middle distance. "But when I saw her bustling out of her cafe back to her other business, I thought, why should her life get to carry on as if nothing's even happened? I was going to lose everything - I *will* lose everything - and she's going to be just as happy without Bill as she would have been with him.

I'm struggling to process all this, numb with shock. My mind feels like it's working through treacle but I slowly manage to make sense of Ivy's rambling. Bill and Maggie were having an affair - and Bill was going to leave his wife for her. *Until Ivy stopped him.* I try to wrench my arm free but Ivy's grip is like a vice and she pulls me closer to her, desperation making her voice shake.

"You understand, don't you? You know how humiliating it is when your husband...and then he said he wanted to leave me!" She laughs. "As if I could bear that. At least the previous affairs were quiet. I could ignore them and we could carry on as if nothing had ever happened. But now - *now!* - he decides it's different, and he wants a fresh start. Well, I wasn't about to let that happen." She nods toward the unsigned divorce papers. "He kept telling me to sign, but I'd told him I just wanted one more Christmas together. Nobody gets divorced at Christmas!"

My stomach turns over as I recall saying those exact words to Jeremy only a few days ago. *But I wouldn't use them as an excuse to commit* murder!

At last, Ivy lets go of me and I watch her pace around the room like some kind of caged animal. She's between me and the door, so I have no way of getting out of here. I sit, trying to think up a way out and watch her closely, straining to hear her as her voice drops to an agitated whisper.

"Of course, I guess it's worked out for the best that I didn't manage to do any serious damage to Maggie. People might have started to ask questions. But now I can continue to be the grieving widow, devastated by my actions...yes, that will certainly win me some sympathy." She smiles, but there's no trace of light in her eyes. "And if I stick close to Maggie as she recovers there's no telling how many other opportunities might come my way. I can wait to get my revenge. I waited twenty years for Bill's." She shakes her head. "If only I'd done it before he squandered all our money."

"Your money?" I ask, almost without meaning to. She glares at me and I shrink into my chair, fumbling together an argument that might placate her enough that I stand a chance of getting out of here. I'd underestimated Ivy. The bruises that I can already feel forming on my arm attest to the strength the small woman possesses. "My husband...ex-husband...*Neil*." I draw in a shaky breath. "He left me in the lurch with our money, too." I kick out one of my feet so that the bell on my elf-slipper jingles. "Why do you think I had to take this humiliating job?"

"Yes, yes, it's very tragic." Ivy's sympathy for our shared predicament is fleeting. Her gaze hardens as she looks at me. "But you're young enough that you can start over. Bill left me with nothing."

There's a miaow and we both look towards the door as a large, fluffy cat strolls into the living room, looking entirely unfazed by the fact that his mistress is in the middle of confessing to murder. Ivy turns back to me, her expression folding into a frown.

"Of course, now you know, I'll have to deal with you, too..." She speaks more to herself than to me, and I change the subject, hoping to keep her talking.

"Is this Snuffy?" I ask, leaning forward in my chair and holding my hand out to the cat. "Is he doing better now? I was talking to Rob - Rob Castle, the vet - about how unwell he's been..."

She softens a little at the mention of her cat and turns away from me just long enough that I manage to get to my feet and make a lunge for the door. She's quicker than I am, though, throwing herself into the doorway before I can pass through it, and blocking me. Her gaze is triumphant, but there's a hardened look in her eyes.

"I knew you didn't care," she spits. "Trying to be all sympathetic, acting as if we have anything in common when it was just a ploy to distract me. Well, I'm sorry, Meredith, but -"

Before she can say a word, the doorbell rings, and we all - Snuffy included - turn towards it. Ivy relaxes her position for just a moment and I reach for the closest thing I can use as a weapon. In one swift movement, I bring down Bill's *Man of the Year award* hard on Ivy's head, holding my breath as she crumples to the floor.

Chapter Thirteen

"And then what happened?"

Kate is sitting next to me on Ivy's over-stuffed sofa, writing down everything I say. Ivy is in the back of a police car outside, under guard, conscious but with a huge lump forming on her head.

"Well, when the doorbell rang I took advantage of her distraction and I - I hit her." I pull down the cuffs of my faded sweater over my shaking hands, recalling the feel of the trophy in my hands and the way it felt to strike the blow that finally incapacitated Ivy. "I hope she isn't badly hurt."

"She'll live," Kate says, drily. She lays one of her hands on mine, patting me warmly. "More importantly, so will you."

"I'm just glad I decided to stop by." Rob strolls in from the kitchen, thrusting a cup of hot chocolate into my hands with a smile. "It's instant, I'm afraid, not a patch on Maggie's." Our eyes meet and I remember the last time he passed me a cup like this. I shudder and he holds tight to the mug until I can safely take it without spilling half of it.

"Yes, why did you?" Kate looks at him.

"Checking up on this little guy." Rob bends down and scoops up Snuffy, who chirrups and nestles deeper into his shoulder. "I decided I should keep up my home visits to him and Mrs. Barraclough, at least until after Christmas. Didn't like the thought of her spending it all alone so soon after losing Bill." He shakes his head. "Of course, if I'd known..."

"Uncle Rob! Where's my hot chocolate?"

"Coming, your highness!" He winks at me, and turns back to the kitchen, taking Snuffy with him. He'd arrived with his niece in tow, and when they'd stumbled upon me, holding Bill's *Man of the Year* award over the body of Ivy Barraclough, he'd leaped into action. Taking the trophy from my hands, he'd bent over Ivy's body, ascertaining she was alive, just unconscious, and somehow made sense of my ranting and railing. His niece had grabbed hold of Snuffy when the cat ran outside, and they'd both come in to wait with me until the police could arrive. When Kate came, he escorted Jess through to the kitchen and made her promise not to leave the table until she'd drawn him the perfect picture of her visit to Santa that morning. He evidently hoped that distracting her and keeping her away from Kate and me would minimize the shock of the day, and I couldn't help agreeing. No little kid should have to think about murder ever - but especially not at Christmas.

"So Ivy killed her husband," Kate mused, flicking back through all the notes she had made on her phone. "And she tried to kill Maggie."

I nod, taking a shaky sip of my powdery hot chocolate.

"Maggie and Bill were having an affair."

"Oh, I know about *that*." Kate smiles ruefully up at me. "In fact, I was beginning to think *Maggie* had been the one who'd killed him because he refused to leave his wife for her." She shudders. "If she hadn't been spending the night in the hospital I would have been on my way to question her about it." She shakes her head. "I can't believe I got it so wrong."

"We all did." I think about how sorry I felt for Ivy Barraclough, and how much of a change had come over her once she'd started confessing to me. I shiver again, wrapping my hands around my warm mug. "She was so angry. She'd held onto a grudge for so long, and even though she and Bill had still stayed married she hadn't forgiven him. She must have been so bitter and miserable for so many years." I think of Neil and the cash he gave me today that's still sitting, untouched, in my pocket. It won't make up for what he's done, but maybe I can look at it as what it was: an attempt to mend fences. *I think when I get home, the first thing I'll do is sign those divorce papers.* I'm not going to hang onto my anger and let it fester the way Ivy did.

"What's wrong?" Kate's looking at me with concern. "You look very serious all of a sudden."

"Oh, I was just thinking...maybe Christmas is a time for fresh starts." I smile, grimly. "And I'm determined to make some."

Kate frowns, but she seems to understand what I mean without me having to explain.

"Good. Just don't do anything *too* radical." She glances around to check we're all alone, then pulls me into her for a hug. "I like you too much the way you are."

I laugh, and she lets me go.

"No, no big changes on the horizon. I just mean, maybe it's time for me to stop letting what happened with Neil overshadow everything good in my life. I have my health, my dignity..." I look down at my elf costume and grimace. "Well, almost. I still have the house, and we've agreed I'll keep it." I drain the last of my hot chocolate. "Maybe I'll get a cat."

"Did you say you want a cat?"

It's as if Rob's been listening, because he reappears in the doorway, holding out Snuffy like some kind of fluffy, squirming trophy.

"I can't take him home on account of my dogs, and I'd hate to see him go to a shelter at Christmas." He pulls a sad face and I can't help but laugh and reach out to take the cat, who leaps out of Rob's arms and onto my lap, where he turns in a circle once and settles down for a snooze, immediately letting out a low, rhythmic purr. "See?" Rob grins. "He likes you."

"What about Ivy?" I ask, stroking Snuffy's head. "I can't just take her cat."

"She'll be staying in police custody for a little while. I'm sure she won't object if she knows he's going to be looked after." Kate winces. "Even if you're the one doing the looking after."

"Don't tell her," Rob says, easily. "Just say I *made arrangements*." He winks at me, and I feel my cheeks heat. I hide my face in Snuffy's fluffy body and think how much cozier my house is going to feel this Christmas with a cat for company.

"Alright, then!" Kate taps the last few notes on her phone, then slides it away. She stands, helping me to my feet, and Snuffy complains a little as his bed gives way beneath him. I hold him tight and he squirms until he's comfortable in my arms. "I guess you're free to go home then, Meredith. Do you need me to give you a ride?"

"No," I say, lifting my head. "I can take care of myself." Snuffy lets out an opinionated little *harrumph* and I smile, knowing that however it feels, I'm not alone anymore.

Epilogue

"And that trophy, the one you used to -"

"Knock out an old woman," Jeremy puts in, helping himself to the roast potatoes.

"Defend yourself." Kate glares at him and turns back to me, holding out the serving bowl of carrots and green beans. "It turns out that the *Man of the Year* award is the very thing she used to kill her husband."

I shudder and spoon a few vegetables onto my plate.

"The lab found traces of blood -"

"We're *eating*," Jeremy reminds her, and Kate swallows the rest of her explanation.

"Anyway, they found the weapon, and now that Ivy's confessed it's all resolved rather neatly. Before my boss comes back, and just in time for Christmas!"

My two friends have decided to spend Christmas Day at my house, and I have to admit, I'm having a wonderful time, even with all the murder talk. Snuffy strolls into the kitchen, already quite at home here, and miaows at us.

"Your dinner is in your bowl!" I remind him, rising from the table to go check he hasn't eaten it all. He hasn't, but there is a tiny space in the center, so I shake the bowl lightly until the whole surface is covered again. "Here you go!" It works for about a minute, and he happily munches away long enough for me to return to my seat.

"Your new house guest is settling in well, then?" Jeremy remarks, pouring so much gravy onto his plate that his vegetables are swimming. "I never thought you were much of a cat person."

"Nor did I," I whisper, certain Snuffy will be able to understand me. I smile. "It's kind of nice, though, having him here. Makes the place feel a bit more lived-in."

"I notice you finally got rid of those divorce papers, too," Kate points out. "Or have you just hidden them out of sight of your nosy friends?"

"No, they're gone." I smile as I recall the weight that lifted from my shoulders once I'd signed them and submitted them to the lawyers before their offices closed for Christmas. "I can firmly draw a line under that whole part of my life."

"Cheers to that!" Jeremy's words are muffled by chewing but he still manages to salute me with his wine glass.

"And cheers to this!" Kate adds, lifting her glass. "You're making life your own, now, and it's going to be great." She smiles. "But here's hoping there are no more murders in the new year."

"No more murders!" Jeremy echoes, clinking his glass against Kate's.

I smile and agree, thinking that I've had enough excitement the past few days to last me solidly into the new year.

Snuffy finishes his meal and comes to wind himself around the legs of our chairs, hoping for some dropped scraps.

"I think I can look forward to a much quieter life from now on," I say, subtly dropping a piece of turkey for my cat to catch. "Just me and my cat."

"And your friends," Kate says, loyally. I smile at her, grateful that she and Jeremy are in my life, grateful that they are here.

"And my friends," I agree, taking a sip of my sparkling wine and thinking how much more enthusiastic I am about the state of my life than I was just a few days ago. I guess if there's one thing the death of Bill Barraclough has taught me it's to be grateful for what I have and to let go of the past. I'm not quite ready to count my ex-husband amongst the friends I'm grateful for, yet, but I'm a little hopeful I might be able to add Rob to the list soon enough. He's stopping by tomorrow to check on Snuffy and I'm planning on sharing some of the Christmas treats that are overflowing out of my cupboards. It's the least I can do to thank him for showing up and saving the day where Ivy was concerned. *Ivy.* My smile falters as I imagine the bleak Christmas Ivy Barraclough will be experiencing. *And she brought it on herself*, I reflect. I shiver, thinking how closely my trajectory had mirrored hers, and am grateful I've been given the chance to course-correct.

"What's wrong?" Kate asks, noticing the change in my demeanor.

"Just thinking," I say, lifting my glass for one more toast. "Here's to Christmas - a time for celebration and goodwill and being grateful for what we have."

Snuffy lets out a contented miaow and curls up underneath the table and I like to think he agrees with me.

The End

About the Author

When Rachel Beattie isn't writing stories, she's usually reading them - especially of the cozy mystery variety. A lifelong devotee of Agatha Christie, she loves putting ze little grey cells to work and is especially fond of anything that can make her laugh while she's collecting a clue or two.

***

Join her mailing list[1] for more information, new release news, exclusives and bonus content.

.

---

1. https://mailchi.mp/003ddbbcc668/newsletter-subscribers

Also by Rachel Beattie

A Serenity Suites Cozy Mystery
Cassie Clinton and the First Fatality
Double Trouble for Cassie Clinton
Cassie Clinton and the Triple Threat

A Slice of Life Cozy Mystery
Love, Lies and Pumpkin Spice
Wed, Dead and Gingerbread
Crime Scenes and Blackcurrant Cream
Spirits, Spells and Caramel
Broken Hearts and Strawberry Tarts
Black Tie and Vanilla Pie
A Slice of Life Cozy Mystery Books 1-3

A Very Merry Murder Mystery
The Santa Slaughter
The First Date Disaster
The Body in the Bookstore

The Harmony Inn Homicide
The Scandal at the Spa
The Babysitter Bungle
The Campground Killer
The Deadly Dinner Party
The Flower Shop Felony
A Very Merry Murder Mystery Books 1-3